Rocket

WIZARD'S BOY

The Potty Panto

Scoular Anderson

A & C Black • London

for Ern and Gaia

Rockets

WIZARD'S BOY - Scoular Anderson

The Muddled Monsters
The Perfect Pizza
The Posh Party
The Potty Panto

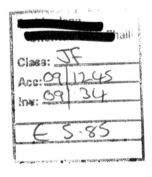

Reprinted 2006, 2007 (twice), 2008
First paperback edition 2000
First published 2000 in hardback by
A & C Black Publishers Ltd
38 Soho Square, London W1D 3HB

www.acblack.com

The right of Scoular Anderson to be identified as author
and illustrator of this work has been asserted by
him in accordance with the Copyright, Designs
and Patents Act 1988.

ISBN 978-0-7136-5224-6

A CIP catalogue record for this book is available
from the British Library.

This book is produced using paper that is made from wood
grown in managed, sustainable forests. It is natural, renewable
and recyclable. The logging and manufacturing processes conform
to the environmental regulations of the country of origin.

Printed and bound by G. Z. Printek, Bilbao, Spain.

CHAPTER 1

Eric Wizzard, the wizard's boy, opened his front door.

Here comes trouble!

LETTERS

He had a bottle of brass polish and a couple of dusters in his hand.

Eric's mum had told him to give the brass door-knocker a good polish. As this was a wizard's house, the door-knocker had something to say about that.

Eric stood back and admired his work.

Then he went across the garden to see
how his dad was doing.

His dad was having trouble with the
lawn mower.

Then Dad said...

That made Eric's heart sink because
his dad wasn't a very good wizard and
his magic rarely did what it was
supposed to do.

His dad cast a spell...

But it grew taller instead.

CHAPTER 2

Eric sat on the doorstep waiting for the people to arrive. Some parents and teachers were going to meet at his house to discuss the end-of-term pantomime.

Maybe we'll do Jack and the Beanstalk.

Eric had been told to keep out of the way but he wanted to see who was coming to the meeting.
His teacher, Miss Perrywinkle, was the first to arrive.

Then Mr Skayles,
who was the
music teacher.

Then Mitchell's mum with Mitchell.

Then Nicko's dad with Nicko.

'You boys amuse yourselves,'
said Eric's mum and the door was shut
for the last time.

So Eric, Nicko and Mitch amused themselves. They kicked a football around the lawn, but the grass was now up to their knees.

They soon went back to sit on the
front doorstep.

Then a voice above them said...

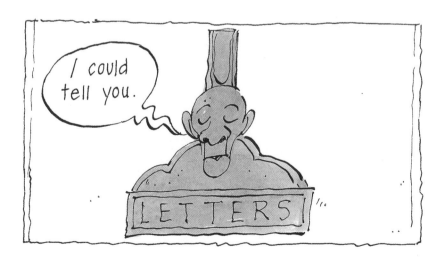

So the door-knocker, who was a bit of a know-it-all, told them...

The door-knocker went on...

They weren't very pleased with what they had been told.

The door-knocker hadn't finished.

Mrs Posh will make the costumes,
Mr Kneesly will be in charge of lighting,
and Mr Wizzard will help with special effects.

SPECIAL EFFECTS!

Eric knew that letting his dad do special effects would only lead to trouble.

At that moment the front door opened, so the boys dived into the long grass. People were leaving.

CHAPTER 3

After school next day, Eric went round to the school hall to see if his dad needed help painting the pantomime scenery...

The Wizzards' dog Theodore was there but Eric couldn't see his dad.

Eric found part of his dad under
a curtain.

His dad had to explain.

Eric set out to look through the school.

He took Theodore with him, just in case.

The classrooms were empty.

The cleaners had arrived and they were making a great racket – enough to scare off an ant-eater.

As Eric passed the head teacher's office he heard her talking to the caretaker.

24

Eric ran back down the
corridor. He had to tell his
dad that the ant-eater
had multiplied.

He bumped into Miss Perrywinkle
outside the hall.

She gave him a piece of paper.

Then Eric saw that Miss Perrywinkle
was staring hard at Theodore.

'Oh dear,' thought Eric. 'If only
Miss Perrywinkle knew the truth!'

CHAPTER 4

When Eric got home, he slumped down on a kitchen chair. He was not happy.

His mum brought him a drink.

Now, Eric's mum was an airline pilot and she was always flying off around the world.

Eric's mum gave him a lift to Emily Sweetbutter's house on the way to the airport.

Emily's mum opened the door. She was eating ice-cream and Eric took a liking to her right away.

Emily was hanging upside-down from a tree in the garden. Eric thought that was a fun thing to do, so he began to relax.

After they had eaten ice-cream...

...and guddled in the pond...

...they sat down to learn their lines.

Eric thought that Emily Sweetbutter was definitely okay.

CHAPTER 5

That evening, Eric's dad propped up Miss Perrywinkle's list of special effects on the kitchen table.

Now, let's see...

This was what it said:

CINDERANNA AND THE UGLY BROTHERS

SPECIAL EFFECTS — for Mr Wizzard.

1 PUFF OF SMOKE — While fairy godmother comes on stage.

2 PUFF OF SMOKE — (as fairy godmother casts spell) to hide cinderanna as she throws dress over her rags.

3 PUFF OF SMOKE — (as fairy godmother casts spell) to hide pumpkin being removed from stage and coach brought on.

4 PUFF OF SMOKE — (as midnight strikes) to hide Cinderanna as she changes from ballgown back to rags.

Many thanks

Miss P.A. Perrywinkle

36

Eric's dad rubbed his hands cheerfully.

And just to prove it, he cast a quick spell. It worked perfectly.

CHAPTER 6

The day of the pantomime arrived and Eric's mum had got home in time. There was great excitement backstage.

39

Eric's dad made wonderful puffs of smoke to hide what was going on on stage.

Soon, it was Eric's turn to go on and dance with Cinderanna at the ball – but he had an attack of nerves.

He was so nervous that he sat in the dressing-room and forgot to put on his costume.

41

He was just about to walk on stage when his dad noticed his clothes. He cast a quick spell...

That made Eric's dance routine with Cinderanna a bit difficult, but Emily didn't bat an eye.

During the next scene Eric tried to calm himself. He knew his dad was up to his usual tricks.

In the last scene, the prince had to put Cinderanna's lost slipper onto her foot but Eric had forgotten to bring the slipper.

Eric's dad came to the rescue again.

But Eric got a kipper instead.

The audience roared with laughter and Emily gave Eric a kiss...

...and the pantomime ended with a wild dance.

Afterwards there was so much excitement that no one asked where the suit of armour had come from.

On the way out Eric overheard
the head teacher talking to
Miss Perrywinkle.

'Thank goodness Dad's magic doesn't last very long!' thought Eric as he headed for the car.